P9-COO-389

Disney's

My Very First Winnie the Pooh™

Tigger's Moving Day

Kathleen W. Zoehfeld Illustrated by Robbin Cuddy

Disney PRESS

NEW YORK

Copyright © 1999 Disney Enterprises, Inc.

All rights reserved. No part of this book may be reproduced or transmitted in any form or by any means, electronic or mechanical, including photocopying, recording, or by any information storage and retrieval system, without written permission from the publisher. For information address Disney Press, 114 Fifth Avenue, New York, New York 10011-5690.

Printed in the United States of America.
Based on the Pooh Stories by A. A. Milne (copyright The Pooh Properties Trust).

FIRST EDITION
1 3 5 7 9 10 8 6 4 2

Library of Congress Catalog Card Number: 98-86431
ISBN: 0-7868-3225-8

Disney's

My Very First Winnie the Pooh

Tigger's Moving Day

After breakfast, Tigger stood up and stretched. "Time for my morning bounce!" he cried.

Sproing! Sproing! Sproing!

"Look out!" cried Rabbit.

Thump! Tigger bumped into one of his cupboards, and his toys came crashing down. "Oooo, that happens every time," he sighed.

"Tigger, you don't have enough bouncing room in this little house," said Rabbit.

Plunk! A toy truck teetered off the shelf and landed on Tigger's head. "Ouch," he sighed, "it's true. But what can I do?"

"We've got to find you a bigger house," declared Rabbit. "That's all there is to it!"

"But . . . " said Tigger.

"No buts," said Rabbit. "I'm going to organize the others right away. Don't worry—we're going to find you a new home!"

By the end of the day, everyone was excited about the big new house they had found for Tigger.

"It IS a bouncy house," said Tigger, "the kind of house Tiggers like best!" He bounced and bounced, and he didn't bump into anything.

"But," he sighed, "I'll miss my old house. And I won't live next door to little Roo anymore. I'll miss him, too."

"I know you'll miss being neighbors with Kanga and Roo," said Christopher Robin, "but now you'll live much closer to me. We can have fun being neighbors—just like you and Roo did."

"Do you like to bounce?" asked Tigger.

"Sometimes," said Christopher Robin.

"Besides, dear," said Kanga, "I promise to bring Roo over to visit, just as often as you like."

"Well, then," said Tigger, perking up a bit. "I hope everyone can stay a while. We can play a game together and eat some cookies."

Tigger opened his new pantry. No cookies.

He opened his new closet. No games.

"Kinda empty, isn't it?" said Eeyore.

"Yeah," agreed Tigger. "Tiggers don't like empty houses. I like my old house better."

Rabbit put his paws on his hips and stared at Tigger. "We aren't finished yet. We need to move all your things from your old house to this house," he said.

"Everything?" asked Tigger.

"Every last little thing," said Rabbit, "and that's a big job, so we'll start first thing tomorrow morning."

Rabbit told everyone to bring their wagons and all the boxes they could find to Tigger's house.

"Wow! Boxes are fun!" cried Roo. "Look at me hiding!!"

Tigger and Roo bounced in and out of boxes.

"There'll be time for fun later," grumbled Rabbit. "Now we've got to pack Tigger's things."

Tigger packed all his games and his stuffed animals in a box. He took his favorite lion out and hugged him. "I want you to stay with me."

Rabbit packed Tigger's dishes.

Kanga packed Tigger's clothes.

Pooh and Piglet packed Tigger's food.

Soon Eeyore arrived with his donkey cart. "We can use this to haul your bigger things," he said helpfully, "furniture and whatnot."

Christopher Robin and Owl hoisted Tigger's bed and table and chairs onto the cart.

Owl and Gopher loaded the boxes on the wagons.

"Time to move it out!" cried Rabbit.

Everyone pulled and pulled.

"Now my new home will be perfect!" cried Tigger, as they unloaded the cart and the wagons and carried everything inside.

"Thanks for your help, everyone," he cried. "Moving was as easy as pie!"

After his friends had gone, Tigger put his toys on his new shelves.

He pushed his bed under the back window, just where he wanted it.

He set his table and chairs in the middle of the big kitchen.

He put his cereal and his extract of malt in his new pantry.

When he was all finished, he sat down to rest.

"Hmmm. Seems like an awfully quiet house," he thought.

He tried out a few bounces, but decided

he wasn't in such a bouncy mood,

after all.

"I sure miss Roo," he sighed.

Just then, Tigger heard a little

voice cry, "Hallooo!"

"Roo!" cried Tigger. "Kanga!

Come on in!"

"We've brought you a bag of cookies," said Kanga.

"Oh, yummy!" cried Tigger.

"Hallooo! Hallooo!" Tigger soon heard all his friends calling outside his new door. Everyone had brought housewarming presents for Tigger.

"Our work's all done," said Rabbit. "Now it's time for fun!"

"Hooray!" cried Tigger and Roo, as they bounced from room to room together, "The kind of fun Tiggers love best!"